The Peace Bridge

by Geof Smith illustrated by Tom McNeely

SCHOLASTIC INC.
New York Toronto London Auckland Sydney
Mexico City New Delhi Hong Kong Buenos Aires

Developed by Kirchoff/Wohlberg, Inc., in cooperation with Scholastic Inc.

 Published by Scholastic Inc. Printed in the U.S.A.
ISBN 0-439-35167-7

2 3 4 5 6 7 8 9 10 24 09 08 07 06 05 04 03

A family trip should be fun, right? Well, not when your family includes my big brother. His name is Allen, and my name is Mike. We're always arguing. He's two years older, and he thinks he's so smart. They should put his picture in the dictionary next to the word "annoying." So, when my parents said we were going to drive to Niagara Falls for our vacation, I knew it would be a long, long drive.

We packed up the car and left early in the morning. We'd barely gone ten miles when Allen started the trouble. First of all, he took up half the back seat with his books. He's always reading. We're only going away for a few days, and he has practically an entire library with him! Next, he started announcing all these dull facts about Niagara Falls to everyone in the car.

"Did you know that Niagara Falls is over twelve thousand years old? They used to be seven miles further down the river, but the water has worn away the earth to its current location."

I rolled my eyes. "If I was interested in falling water, I would have spent the vacation in the shower."

"It's too bad you didn't," Allen said.

"It is too bad I had to come. I wanted to go to Yosemite Park in California. If we had gone there, we could have seen bears and gone camping. That would have been a much better vacation."

"Well, we aren't going there, but if you get out now and start walking you might get there in a year."

We started wrestling. Allen has longer arms and got a good grip on me, but I'm pretty strong and wriggled away.

Mom spun around and glared at us from the front seat. "Allen! Michael! Stop it! Sit still."

Dad didn't say anything. He just kept staring at the road and driving.

Things were calm for a while. I watched six mile-posts pass by. Then Allen opened his window, and wind started blowing on my face. I asked him to roll it up a bit, but he only opened it more. I could deal with that, but I didn't like it when he leaned over and told me my car list was wrong. I always make a list of cool cars that we pass on car trips. I know my cars very well, and there's no way my list was wrong. We started to wrestle again. Dad told us to quit it. He didn't yell—he didn't have to. After that we were quiet . . . until lunch.

We drove all day, and some time after dinner we reached our hotel, which was just outside Buffalo. Mom and Dad had one room, and Allen and I had another one. A door connected our rooms. When Mom checked in on us, Allen and I were fighting about who would get which bed.

"Oh, would you two please stop all this silly fighting?" My mom looked tired after the long day. "Is one bed really better than the other?"

"Nope," I said quickly. My mother looked surprised. I felt surprised that I said it.

"Listen, this isn't just your vacation. It's also your father's and mine. You guys seem to enjoy fighting, but we don't like it. We'd like a little peace and quiet."

Allen and I both studied our shoes. I felt two feet tall.

"Listen," my mother said, "I'll make a deal with you two. If you two can make it through this trip without another fight, I'll get you each a present. Maybe a computer game for you, Allen—and how about a new skateboard for you, Mike?"

Allen and I nodded. A new skateboard should have made me happy, but it didn't. Allen looked pretty far from excited, too.

Why did I fight over a bed I didn't want? It's like I just wanted to fight with Allen, and that didn't really make sense.

As we left Buffalo the next day, Allen and I looked at the postcards we got in the hotel. One of them had a bridge on it. Mom explained that it was the Peace Bridge. It had been built to show the friendship between Canada and the United States.

Dad said, "You boys might think a Peace Bridge of your own would be a good idea." We both pretended we didn't hear him.

Finally, we made it to the Falls. I have to admit they were really impressive. We all stood against a railing and stared, our mouths hanging open. Falling water thundered in the air around us, and foam and mist boiled nearly two hundred feet below. Then my brother started talking.

"There are actually three sets of falls—the American, the Bridal Veil, and the Horseshoe. The Horseshoe Falls are huge. Did you know that some people went over the Horseshoe Falls in a barrel?"

Mom and Dad seemed interested, but I thought the Falls didn't need any narration. It was like Allen wanted to be more important than the Falls.

"I wish we could send you over the Falls in a barrel," I said.

"I'd like to see you try," Allen said.

Allen and I almost started fighting, but at the last second we froze. Mom and Dad didn't have to say anything. I have to admit, I was proud of myself.

We walked towards the Falls. There were a series of narrow stairways that wound along the cliffs so you could get even closer to the crashing water.

Allen leaned closer to me and said, "It's not going to be easy not fighting, is it?"

I shook my head.

"Well, I have an idea."

"You usually do," I replied.

"Listen," Allen said, "I have these two rubber bands. We'll each put one around our wrist. Here." He put one on, and I did the same. "Whenever I feel like fighting, I'll snap it against my wrist. If you feel like fighting, you snap yours."

"You mean, if I want to fight I should snap your wrist." I reached over, stretched his band, and let it slap him. He winced.

"No," he said, "If you feel like fighting, you snap your own band. Like this." He plucked my band and let it sting me. "This way we'll remind ourselves to keep our tempers under control. Then we'll get those presents. Okay?"

"I'll give it a try," I said, and we jogged to catch up with Mom and Dad.

The catwalks brought us closer and closer to the crashing water. The air was damp with spray, and the Falls roared like a non-stop explosion. Up close you could really feel the power of the Falls. I started thinking that coming here wasn't such a bad idea . . . but I'd never tell my brother. I didn't want him to know that I was terrified, even if I liked being scared.

Then Allen went and ruined the moment. He started talking about how they generated electricity from the falling water. I was about to say that the biggest generator in the area was his mouth, but I stopped myself.

I gave the rubber band a little snap. It didn't really hurt, but it did make me pause. Mom and Dad were having a fine time, and so was Allen. Why should I ruin it for everyone? I kept quiet.

I listened to him tell us that the Cave of Winds wasn't really a cave, but an elevator and a bunch of tunnels. It was like we were sneaking into a secret fortress. Attendants gave us plastic yellow slickers. Finally, we stepped outside. We were very close to the Falls!

White, foaming water cascaded down in front of us. Spray billowed up in front of us. I could almost reach out and touch the crashing water.

I noticed out of the corner of my eye that Allen snapped his rubber band. It was nice to know that he was trying, too.

Dad patted me on the back. "This is pretty awesome, isn't it, Mike?" He was practically yelling to be heard over the gushing water.

"Sure is," I said. I don't know if he heard me, but he couldn't miss the big smile on my face.

That night we ate dinner at a restaurant that overlooked the American Falls. Giant colored lights shone on the water, but it was complete darkness at the bottom. It was like the water was falling into outer space.

Dad suggested we get some appetizers, and right away Allen said, "Let's get stuffed mushrooms!"

He knows I don't like mushrooms, and he always orders them for that reason.

"Mushrooms are fungi," I said. "What kind of creep eats fungi?"

"The only reason you know that they're fungi," Allen said, "is because I told you."

I was about to fire back another insult, but I shut my mouth and snapped my rubber band. I heard Mike snap his band too. That made me laugh, and he started giggling, too. After that it was all quiet at the dinner table front. We got stuffed mushrooms and mozzarella sticks. There was no need to fight after all.

The next morning we went on a boat called the Maid of the Mist. Allen said this would be the best part of the trip. I don't know how he knew this since he'd never done it before, but I didn't open my mouth. I didn't even have to snap my rubber band. I was getting good at being good.

We climbed aboard a giant boat, and we were given those yellow ponchos again. When the engines started, I felt the vibrations right through my feet and up my legs. The boat chugged right towards the crashing wall of water. We kept getting closer and closer. We practically cruised right under the waterfall.

Waves rocked the boat. Thunder roared all around us. Allen and I stayed on the deck, but Mom and Dad went back into the cabin. I had to tip my head all the way back to see the top of the waterfall. Spray rained down on my face.

"This is the best part of the trip," I laughed. "Did you say that people rode in barrels over that thing?"

"Yes."

"Wow!" I said. "That's crazy."

"You know what? There was once a tightrope-walker who went across from America to Canada. He even carried passengers on his shoulders!"

"That's outrageous!" I exclaimed.

The boat rocked, and I started to fall. Allen grabbed me. "We don't want you going into the water . . . at least not without a barrel."

Allen is always spouting facts, and it usually seems like showing off. This time he was just telling me things he thought were cool. You know, sharing. That didn't really bug me. In fact, I liked it. When we got back on land, and dried off a little, we walked around taking pictures.

Our vacation was almost over. Next morning, we repacked our bags and loaded up the car. As we left Buffalo, we caught a glimpse of the Peace Bridge.

"It's pretty cool," I said.

The sun was shining, and the river glittered beneath the steel beams.

There was a little wind blowing. "It's amazing that Canada and the United States would build a bridge as a sign of the peace between them. It's amazing that we can cross it so easily. How'd they ever build it?"

Allen shrugged. "I don't know."

"You don't? That's nice for a change."

Mom came up from behind and draped her arms over our shoulders. "You guys have been really good, and I haven't forgotten our deal. Peace is wonderful between countries, and between brothers."

We just looked at each other.

"Don't worry, Mom," Allen said, "you won't have to bribe us again."

Mom looked really surprised. "Do you have anything to say about this, Mike?"

"Nahh, I guess he's right," I said and snapped my rubber band.

As usual, I knew Allen was right, and as usual, there was no way I was going to admit it.

Allen looked at me and said, "Do you think we can keep this up until we get home?"

"I can, but I doubt you can do it."

"Oh, is that a challenge?"

Dad snapped a picture right at that moment. Allen and I look like we're fighting, but we're really having a good time.